THE MYSTERY OF THE MISSING TREASURE

THE
MYSTERY
OF THE
MISSING TREASURE

Janet Lorimer

A LUCAS · EVANS BOOK

AN
APPLE
PAPERBACK

SCHOLASTIC INC.
New York Toronto London Auckland Sydney

ISBN 0-590-43479-9

12 11 10 9 8 7 6 5 4   3 4/9

Printed in the U.S.A.   40

For my mother,
Margaret Grahame Collins,
with all my love and gratitude.

1

Captain Scalawag's treasure! It was the first thing Pete thought of when he woke up. He jumped out of bed and began pulling on his clothes. Gold and jewels! Pete's eyes gleamed. Today he was going to pry the whole story out of his new friend, Danny Butcher — or else!

Pete couldn't understand why Danny didn't think a story about lost treasure was exciting. Maybe it was because Danny had grown up with the story, but Pete was a newcomer to Oak Bluff. And so far, that treasure story was the only thing Pete liked about this dumb town.

For an instant he shut his eyes and tried to pretend he was back in the city. The memory of city noise and city smells, of crowded sidewalks, strange shops, and the hustle and bustle of traffic made him homesick. His parents had agreed that if Pete wanted to visit his old friends, he could spend Thanksgiving vacation in the city. But that was months away. Meanwhile he was stuck in this little town with no friends — except Danny. To top it off, he'd had to give up everything he really liked doing. His roller skates were useless now; Oak Bluff didn't have a roller rink. He couldn't continue with judo because no classes were held. Today he and Danny were going swimming, but Danny said they swam in the river because the town didn't have a pool.

"It figures!" Pete muttered. He ran a comb through his hair and tried hard not to think about it. Like it or not, Oak Bluff was his new home.

Pete went downstairs. In the kitchen his mother was cooking breakfast, trying to avoid tripping over cartons of dishes and cutlery. His father was gulping down a cup of coffee, nervous on this first day at his new job. Pete's older sister, Jessica, was unpacking the silverware.

"I'll be so glad when we have everything put away," Mrs. Whitney said, as Pete slid into his place at the table. "Good morning, Pete. You're up early. Ready to unpack more boxes?"

"Oh, Mom!" Pete groaned. "Do I have to? Danny

said he'd take me swimming today. Can't I just have one day off?"

"Well. . . ." Mrs. Whitney smiled. "I guess you do deserve a break."

"Me, too, Mom," Jessica said. "Bob Morris asked me to have lunch with him today."

"Da cops, da cops, here come da cops!" Pete chanted.

Jessica glared at him. "Bob is not 'cops,' Pete. He's a deputy sheriff, and I'd appreciate it if you'd try to act your age for a change."

Pete made a face at her. Sisters! Just because Jessica was eighteen, she thought she was such a big shot.

"I have to go," Mr. Whitney said. "I can't believe I'll be in my office in fifteen minutes, instead of fighting traffic for an hour. Moving to the country was the smartest thing we ever did."

After her husband left, Mrs. Whitney brought her coffee cup to the table. "I'm going to spend the day in the attic," she said. "That place is a treasure trove!"

"A what?" The word *treasure* caught Pete's attention.

"I don't mean gold and jewels," Mrs. Whitney

laughed. "Are you still thinking about Captain Scalawag's treasure?"

Pete flushed. His family wouldn't laugh if he did find it. He could just picture the headlines! *TWELVE-YEAR-OLD FINDS LOST TREASURE! CENTURY-OLD MYSTERY SOLVED BY NEWCOMER!* Pete grinned to himself. He'd be a hero! And, best of all, he'd be rich! Then maybe he could talk his parents into moving back to the city.

Of course, he'd have to find the treasure first. And in order to find it, Pete had to know more about it.

"Mom, the guy who hid the treasure, why was he called Captain Scalawag? Was that his real name?"

"No, it was a nickname. A scalawag is a scamp or a rascal, and that's what people started calling him long afterward. Oh, Pete, before you go swimming, I want you to move some of these boxes out to the porch."

Peter looked at the cardboard boxes of ancient pottery and cooking utensils. He poked into one with his finger, dislodging a spider.

"This is junk! What're you going to do with it?"

"Junk! Look again, Pete. See those sadirons?"

Pete picked up the old-fashioned iron. It was

very small but so heavy he had trouble lifting it. "This is an iron?"

"That's right. Women owned several and heated them on top of a wood stove. So when one cooled down, another was ready to use."

"But they're so heavy!"

"Maybe that's why they called them sadirons," Jessica said. "Having to iron with them would make anyone sad." She picked up one of the irons and made a face. "Whew! No wonder those women grew old before their time. Mom, look at this kettle! Couldn't we use it? It's so antique-looking." She tried to lift it from the box as she spoke, but dropped it back with a grunt.

"Here, let me do that," Peter said. "You're really out of shape, Jess."

Jessica's mouth tightened. "Go ahead! You try to lift it."

Pete tried and failed. "Wow! That's heavy!"

"Now who's out of shape?" Jessica looked smug. Pete made a face at her. Jessica ignored him. "Where did you find all this stuff, Mom?"

"Your father found it in the barn. The family who owned this house kept everything. It's amazing what I've come across, especially in the attic."

Their real estate agent had told the Whitneys

that the house had been in the Hatler family from the time it was built, in the 1850's, until recently when the last Hatler, Miss Maudie Hatler, a spinster, died. There was no one to inherit the house, so it had been sold, complete with furniture and other household items.

"This house is full of antiques," Mrs. Whitney said. "I'm hoping to sell a lot of them to some of the antique dealers in the city."

Pete thought this talk about antiques was boring. He began moving the boxes to the porch and had finished by the time Danny arrived.

Pete and Danny were the same age. Danny, the son of their real estate agent, had mentioned the treasure the first time the boys had met, probably hoping to impress Pete. It had worked! Pete was now determined to get Danny to give him more details.

"You ready to go?" Danny asked.

"Hold on, I've got to get my towel." Pete hurried upstairs to let his mother know he was leaving. He found her sitting in the middle of the attic, sorting through a box of old papers. She had dust on her face and cobwebs in her hair.

"Pete, look what I found!"

"Mom, Danny's waiting. I've got to go."

"This will only take a minute. Here is an old journal that the first owner, Lena Hatler, kept. Listen: *'Caught Zeb Tyler and Willy Coates in the apple orchard again. Warned them I would skin them alive if they stole any more of my apples.'* She wrote that on June 19, 1864, over a hundred years ago."

Pete squirmed. "Mom, I really have to go."

"Oh, Pete," his mother sighed. "I wish you were more interested in history. Just think of it! Boys stealing apples a century ago. People don't really change much, do they?"

"What happened to the apple orchard?" Pete asked, pretending to be interested.

"Oh, it's long gone, I'm afraid. But I believe it used to be on that slope behind the house. There are just a few old stumps left. Don't you think that's interesting?"

"Yeah, Mom, but I — "

" — have to go. I know." She sighed again. "But be careful. Watch out for snakes, and don't get sunburned, and. . . ."

But Pete was already gone.

2

"**O**kay, Danny, you promised to tell me all about that lost treasure," Pete said, as the boys left the house.

"Don't tell me you think you can find it." Danny laughed.

"Why not? Did you ever look for it?"

"Are you nuts? Old Miss Hatler wouldn't let anyone near her place!"

"Miss Hatler? The old lady who owned our place last?"

"That's right. The treasure's supposed to be hidden somewhere on your property."

Pete stared at Danny. "You never told me that before."

Danny shrugged. "So what? People went over the place with a fine-tooth comb years ago."

"Wait a minute," Pete said. "Start at the beginning. All I know is that some guy named Captain Scalawag hid some jewels and gold but no one ever found them. Just where did he get this treasure?"

"Okay," Danny said, "I'll start over. It was during the Civil War. You know, the war between the states."

"I studied all that in school," Pete said. "What does the Civil War have to do with Oak Bluff? This is California and California wasn't in the war."

"No, but a lot of people living here were from the South," Danny said. "They still had families and friends there, and things were pretty tough. The North was winning the war, and the South was running out of food and other supplies. So a lot of people here in Oak Bluff were worried. Anyway, this guy — his real name was Seth Delaney — he came to Oak Bluff in a beat-up old wagon full of stuff he was trying to sell. You know, like a peddler."

Pete nodded.

"He had a lame old horse and wasn't making any money because most towns already had stores that sold everything he was trying to sell. He said he'd been a captain in the Confederate Army, but he got shot and couldn't fight anymore. Mrs. Lena Hatler felt sorry for him and gave him a job as a hired hand on her farm. She was a widow and needed help running her place.

"Well, the captain — that's what they called him, even if he wasn't in the army anymore — the captain started telling people what it was like in the South, with the war and all. He really upset them with his stories. Then he told them that if they really wanted to help, they should get as much money together as they could, and he'd help them smuggle it to their people. The money would buy food and medicine and stuff like that."

"And they believed him?" Pete hooted with laughter.

"Are you kidding? They gave him everything they could. Of course most of them were poor farmers and didn't have much. But the women gave him jewelry — you know, like their wedding rings. And some of the men borrowed money from the bank."

"Boy, that was dumb!" Pete shook his head. "So how come they think he buried it?"

"Well, they caught him trying to sneak out of Oak Bluff. When they searched his wagon, they couldn't find the treasure, so they figured he must have buried it."

"Couldn't they make him tell where he'd hidden it?" Pete asked.

Danny laughed. "Oh, they tried. They even threatened to hang him, but the captain didn't believe them. He just laughed. I guess that made them so mad they got carried away, and they really did hang him."

Pete whistled. "Then what?"

"Then they went out to the Hatler place, looking for it. They tore up Mrs. Hatler's garden and her flower beds, and they even tried digging up the floor of her barn. Boy, was she mad! She told them if they ever came back she'd shoot them full of buckshot!"

"If no one ever found it, it has to be there," Pete said. "I think we should try to find it."

"Are you kidding? There's acres and acres of land! What are you going to do, dig it up foot by foot? That'd take forever!"

"There must be some way to find it," Pete said.

"Oh, yeah? Well, good luck. Look, there's the river."

They had reached the bottom of the bluff. A

group of kids, some Pete's age, some younger, had already gathered to swim. As Pete and Danny approached, the other kids stopped talking.

Pete laid his towel in the sand under a pine tree. He had his trunks on under his jeans, and he laid his jeans, T-shirt, and watch on top of the towel. As he looked up, he noticed several kids looking at his watch enviously.

"Who's the new guy?" he heard someone ask Danny.

"Pete Whitney. His folks have the Hatler place." A few of the boys nodded to Pete and he nodded back, feeling self-conscious and not liking it.

Suddenly, and with a good deal of splashing, a large, chunky boy lumbered out of the water. He had blond hair; small, pale eyes; and a tough expression. "Where are you from?" he asked, looking Pete up and down.

Pete told him. The chunky boy grinned and spat into the water. "Flatlander, huh?" He didn't make it sound like a compliment.

Pete was angry. Why was this country hick making fun of his city background? "So what's it to you?" he sneered.

Danny edged toward Pete. "Hey, take it easy," he said. "That's Duffy Snell."

"That supposed to mean something?" Pete asked, not bothering to lower his voice.

"Come on, knock it off." Danny sounded annoyed. Pete knew he was overreacting, but he didn't care. He was fed up with being treated like something under a microscope. And now he was supposed to bow down before the local bully? No way! Pete thought about some of the street gangs back home. Now *they* were tough! But this overgrown hunk of lard? Pete could barely keep from laughing.

"Think you're really big, don'tcha?" Duffy sneered.

Pete ignored him and walked to the edge of the water. The river was wide and green, rippling slowly along between low banks. "So this is where you swim," he said to Danny.

"Take it easy when you go in," Danny warned. "It's pretty cold."

"Oh, yeah?" Pete stuck one foot in the water. "Yow! That *is* cold!"

The other boys laughed. Even Danny grinned. "Well, don't say I didn't warn you. The river's melted snow from high up in the mountains. It's like that all year. Let's swim awhile and then I'll show you the drop."

"What's that?"

"Up there." Danny pointed to a gigantic boulder that loomed out over the river. Some of the kids had already climbed to the top. A rope had been tied to an overhanging branch and everyone took turns swinging out over the river, then dropping into the water.

"Hey, that looks all right," Pete said.

"Yeah, well, it's a little tricky," Danny said.

"Are you kidding? Where I used to swim, at the Y, we had a diving board twice as high as that!"

"Big deal!" Duffy snorted. Pete whirled around.

"You talking to me?"

"I ain't talking to the rocks, city boy!" Duffy grinned, but the smile never reached his eyes.

"Listen, punk," Pete said angrily, "lay off!"

"Pete — " Danny began, but neither Pete nor Duffy paid any attention.

"Think you're pretty tough, don'tcha?" Duffy laughed. "But I bet you get up on that rock and chicken out!"

"You're on!" Once the words were out of his

mouth, Pete had no way out. "How do I get up there?" he said, trying to sound confident.

Danny showed Pete how to climb up the back side of the boulder. Pete walked out across the nearly flat surface and looked down into the deep green pool of water below. It was ringed by a wall of rocks that rose like jagged teeth just beneath the surface. The drop was no more than twelve feet, but from the top of the boulder, looking down, it seemed to go on forever. This wasn't going to be as simple as he had thought.

Pete felt Duffy's beefy hand clamp down on his shoulder. "Well? Wanna quit?"

"No way!" Pete was determined to show this bully that city kids weren't sissies.

Duffy grinned and licked his lips. "Okay, here's the deal. The guy who drops closest to the rocks is the winner."

Pete gulped. "Okay!" he said. "You go first!"

Duffy snorted with laughter. "Move aside." He grabbed the rope and, with a running jump, swung far out over the river. As the rope swung back, Duffy dropped. For a second, Pete thought he was going to smash on the rocks, but his body hit the water and just missed them. He disappeared beneath the surface. There was a moment of silence, then he reappeared, gasping for breath, churning the water with his big arms.

Duffy grinned up triumphantly at Pete. "Okay, city boy," he shouted, "now it's your turn." He swam across the pool to the group of admiring watchers. Now all eyes turned on Pete and everyone grew silent.

Pete grabbed the rope. His hands were slippery. One at a time he wiped them down the sides of his trunks. He looked straight ahead, out across the water, trying not to see those jagged rock teeth waiting to impale him.

He took a deep breath, backed up as far as he could, and began running. He swung through the air, and the world tilted. He felt dizzy, but resisted an urge to shut his eyes. The hungry green monster with its open jaws was waiting!

He flew out across the water and up, up to the limits of the arc. Then he was back, his stomach dropping as if on an elevator ride. The rock teeth seemed to snap at his feet as he flew over them. A split second later, he let go!

Pete fell through the air with sickening speed and hit the water. The icy river closed over his head as he plummeted down. His feet slammed against the sandy bottom, jolting his body, but he pushed hard off the river floor, knifing upward. His lungs felt ready to burst. He had to breathe! Where was the surface?

Then, just as he could stand it no longer, he broke free into air and sunshine. There was a rush of sound. Everyone was yelling. Pete's heart was pounding in his ears and his breath exploded in gasps. He turned weakly onto his stomach and swam to shore.

Danny reached out to help him out of the water. "That was great, Pete!"

"Who won?" Pete gasped.

"It was a tie," Danny said.

A tie! Pete was relieved until he turned to look at Duffy. From the expression on the bully's face, Pete knew, with a sinking feeling, that his troubles with Duffy were far from over.

3

"How much farther?" Pete panted. The boys had decided to walk into town after they finished swimming. Pete, who was used to riding a bus everywhere in the city, was feeling every step. The sun felt so hot and dust rose to choke him. Score another point against Oak Bluff!

"Not far," Danny answered. "Look, there's Main Street. Let's get a hamburger and a Coke and watch them setting up for the Fourth of July."

"You mean we have to go all the way to the fairgrounds?" Pete moaned.

"No, just into town. On the Fourth we have a kind of play on Main Street."

"Really?"

Danny pointed to a huge oak. Below its spreading branches, workmen were constructing a crude stage.

"Tell me about the play," Pete said, as the boys collapsed onto the wooden steps, grateful for the shade.

"Well, back in 1864, on the Fourth of July, everyone was in town celebrating. That's when the captain tried to sneak out, only someone spotted him at the Hatler place. He was loading up his wagon and getting ready to leave. When the people found out what he was up to, a whole bunch of them went after him. They brought him back to town and put him in the jail. But when they couldn't find the treasure in his wagon, they dragged him out to Main Street and hung him."

Pete gave a weak whistle to show Danny he was listening. Actually he could barely concentrate because his head was beginning to ache so badly.

"So every year we put on a play that tells the story," Danny went on. "The people in town take different roles, and the drama teacher at the high school directs it. It's pretty good. The tourists sure eat it up."

"Really?" Pete said. But he was barely listening. His head was beginning to whirl and his stomach felt queasy.

"Hey, you kids better go somewhere else," one

of the workmen ordered. We're pretty busy here and you're going to be in the way."

"Okay," Danny said. He stood up. "Come on, Pete, let's go get something to eat."

Pete tried to stand up, but suddenly his knees gave in. He heard a rushing sound in his ears. The world seemed to pitch and turn, and then there was nothing but darkness.

Pete heard voices, at first a distant babble, then coming closer, getting louder, more distinct.

"Is he hurt?"

"Hard to tell. Better get the doctor."

". . . boy just collapsed. I picked him up, brought him in here. . . ."

"Where's his ma? Someone better fetch. . . ."

Pete opened his eyes and saw faces looming over him. He blinked, bringing them into focus.

He was in a large, unfamiliar room with shelves on the walls and a counter with large barrels in front of it. The shelves were stacked with goods. A store! Pete shook his head, trying to remember what had happened. He felt a cool hand on his forehead. "Easy, now, the doctor is on his way."

Then Pete remembered. Swimming, the long walk into town, the terrible heat. . . .

"Where is he? Where is my boy?" It was the frightened voice of a woman. "Is he hurt? Look at me, son."

Pete stared at the face of a total stranger. The woman knelt on the floor beside him. "Oh, Zeb, what a fright you gave me!"

Pete looked at her in disbelief. *Zeb?*

A burly man pushed his way through the crowd. "Now calm down, Mrs. Tyler, there's no sense carrying on like that. You'll just scare the boy. Well, Zeb, how do you feel? Any pain?"

Pete was so shocked he couldn't speak. Who were these weird people? And why did they call him Zeb?

As the doctor examined him, Pete had a chance to look around. He was in a store, all right, but it was not like any store he'd ever seen before. And the people! They weren't dressed like anyone he'd ever met. The women wore long dresses, and the men looked like they'd just stepped out of an old western movie.

Pete struggled to sit up. Through the door he could see a wide dirt street. There were no sidewalks. And no cars! Boardwalks were in front of the buildings, and horses were in the street. Where was he, anyhow?

Pete began to panic. Suddenly he couldn't breathe. He gasped, trying to pull air into his lungs.

"Easy, boy, lie back down. You . . . bad fall . . . rest. . . ."

The words slowed, blurred, and darkness whirled around him. Pete was falling, falling. . . .

"Is he hurt, doctor?"

The familiar voice of his father broke through the roaring in his ears. Pete opened his eyes. "Dad?"

"Pete, how do you feel?"

"Kind of weak. Boy, am I glad to see you!"

Mr. Whitney smiled. "You had us worried, son."

Another face loomed over Pete. A stranger's face, but this time the clothing was familiar.

"Hello, Pete. I'm a doctor."

After a thorough examination, the doctor decided that Pete was suffering from heat exhaustion. "You've got one heck of a sunburn," the doctor grinned. "But other than that, you're okay. You'd better rest for a day or two and drink lots of liquids. And above all, stay out of the sun till that burn heals."

"Let's go home," Mr. Whitney said. "I called your mother and she's pretty worried. Matter of fact, you gave Danny quite a scare, too."

As his father helped him off the examining table, Pete asked. "Who brought me here?"

"The men working on the stage," Mr. Whitney said. "It's a good thing the doctor's office is just across the street. They brought you right over here. When Danny told them who you were, they called me right away."

"Wait a minute!" Pete said. "Before they brought me here, I was in a store."

Pete's father and the doctor looked puzzled. "What are you talking about, Pete?" his father asked.

"I woke up in a store," Pete said. "Everyone was wearing funny clothes. I guess they must be rehearsing for that Fourth of July play."

"Pete, I don't know what you're talking about. There's no store on this end of Main Street," Mr. Whitney said.

"Sounds like you had quite a dream," the doctor added.

"No! It happened. It was real. Don't you believe me, Dad?"

"Calm down, Pete," Mr. Whitney said. "Sometimes dreams seem very real to us. But believe me, that's all it was."

"But there must be a store!" Pete could not believe he'd dreamed it.

"As a matter of fact," the doctor said, "there was a store right here where my office is now. It was the old General Mercantile. But it burned down, oh, forty or fifty years ago."

"See, Dad!"

"Now wait a minute," Mr. Whitney said. "I bet I can explain that. Your mother and I were talking about the history of this town just the other day. You probably overheard us, and that was why you dreamed about it."

"You and Mom never talked about a store. Did you know there was a store here?" Pete demanded.

"Well, no. . . ." Mr. Whitney paused, frowning. "No, but — "

"Then how could I know that if you didn't?"

"Okay, Pete, that's enough!" His father sounded tired. "I'm not going to argue with you. You had a dream, that's all. Let's get home so you can rest. I have to get back to the office."

Pete was quiet all the way home. It wasn't fair! Grown-ups always got the last word. No matter what his father said, Pete did not believe he'd had a dream. But then, he wondered, if he hadn't had a dream, what had *really* happened to him?

4

Pete stayed indoors for the next few days. He did not talk about his "dream" again, but it was still very much on his mind. It was so vivid — the way the store smelled, the feel of rough boards, the jingling of horses' harnesses, and the creak of leather. Pete had never "dreamed" smells and sounds before.

He was willing to believe that part of his dream was based on things he had already been told. His mother had mentioned Zeb Tyler just that morning, and Danny had told him a lot about Oak Bluff's history. Pete had had it on his mind, so it could have been a dream. But the part about the store didn't fit. He hadn't even known it existed. Still, he couldn't explain what had happened.

Being inside all day was making him bored and restless. And Pete was very happy when his mother finally came to his rescue. "Too bad you aren't interested in those journals I found," she said, her eyes twinkling. "I've been reading them and I found more about Captain Scalawag!"

"You did? What did you find out?"

"Oh, fascinating things," she teased. "Why don't you read them? It'll give you something to do."

Pete glanced at the spidery handwriting and faded ink. "Oh, Mom, I don't want to read all that. Can't you tell me what you found?"

"Well, I guess I could. Of course I still have a lot of unpacking to do. And it takes so much time."

Pete sighed. "I get the message. Okay, I'll unpack, you talk!"

Mrs. Whitney thumbed through the pages. "Listen to this, Pete: *'Captain Delaney tells us the war is fought by boys, some as young as ten. My son Tom will be seven come March. I can scarce believe that children are being conscripted into the Army.'* "

"Ten!" Pete stared at his mother.

"There's more! *'The soldiers fear the doctors as much as they fear the enemy. Medicines are in short supply. Disease runs rampant and conditions are primitive.'* "

"Oh, yuck!"

27

"They didn't have antibiotics in those days," Mrs. Whitney reminded Pete. "Next time the doctor gives you a shot, be grateful!" Then she continued: " *The Confederate dollar is worthless. The price of food is so high and everything is in such short supply. Yankee soldiers show no mercy. They take what they can carry to feed themselves and their fellow soldiers. What they cannot carry, they destroy. Army deserters roam the country like packs of wild animals.'* "

"So that's why the people of Oak Bluff wanted to send their money to the South," Pete said. "Boy, the captain really conned them." Then, remembering Zeb Tyler, he reached for the journal. "Where's that part you read the other day? About the kids stealing apples?"

Mrs. Whitney thumbed back and forth till she found the passage. She read it aloud. Then she turned a few pages. "Here's something else about Zeb Tyler. *'The Tylers lost their son Zeb last night. He sickened with the cholera a week ago and lingered till last evening when he took a turn for the worse. Paid a call on the Tylers this afternoon. Poor Mrs. Tyler is beside herself with grief. Zeb was her youngest and such a rascal, but I couldn't fault the boy. His Mama did spoil him so. I thought of him and Willy Coates stealing those apples from my orchard. Wish Zeb was alive. I would take him all the apples he could eat.'* " Mrs. Whitney put the journal down, a thoughtful look on her face. "How sad! So many children died in those days."

"How old was he, Mom?"

"Let's see. This is dated July 11, 1864. He was twelve, Pete. Just your age."

Pete was shocked. "What is chol— that thing you said?"

"Cholera? It was a terrible disease." She sighed. "Every time someone talks about the good old days, I wonder! Some things just weren't so good."

Before they could read more of the journal, Pete's father came home. "Pete, do you feel up to taking a look in the barn and some of those sheds with me?"

"Sure!" Pete jumped up, grateful for a chance to get out of the house.

As they crossed the yard to the sagging old sheds, Mr. Whitney said, "Be careful poking around in there. There may be snakes."

"I'm not afraid of snakes," Pete scoffed.

"I'm talking about rattlers," Mr. Whitney warned. "I understand they can get pretty big

29

and mean. I don't want you to be afraid of them, just show a healthy respect."

"Dad, do we have to clean out all these old sheds? They're so full of junk!"

Mr. Whitney grinned. "Antiques, Pete. That's what your mother calls them."

"Well, if Mom likes them so much, why doesn't she clean that stuff out?"

"Your mother has enough to do in the house. I want to see if we can use the old barn for a garage this winter. Some of the sheds are really in bad shape, though. I'm afraid we'll have to tear them down." He opened one of the sheds. "Look at that!" He whistled. "There's a lot of wood in here. It'll make nice fires in our fireplace this winter."

"Look, Dad — horseshoes! There must be hundreds of them."

"Not hundreds," Mr. Whitney corrected. "But a lot. Don't forget, the Hatlers — "

" — never threw anything away," Pete finished. "But where'd they get so many?"

"I suppose they did their own blacksmithing. Look what else I found." Mr. Whitney lifted a pile of moldy gunnysacks, revealing several small clay pots underneath. "Know what I think those are?

Old crucibles. They were used for melting metals. I bet they even had their own forge!"

"Why would they need crucibles?"

"Beats me! That's why I'm not a blacksmith." He grinned. "But look at this." Mr. Whitney pointed to a large metal cauldron farther back in the shed. "Mrs. Hatler probably used this for cooking or making candles. Over there is an old churn. And wait till you see what's in that barrel! Nails, more horseshoes, some old axe heads, some — "

"All right, Dad! I've seen enough. I still say it's all junk!"

"One man's junk is another man's treasure," Mr. Whitney laughed. "Let's go look in the barn."

"Speaking of treasure," Pete said, "did you know that Captain Scalawag hid his treasure right here on our property?"

Mr. Whitney listened with interest while Pete repeated everything Danny had told him. "Where do you suppose it could be, Dad?"

"Oh, Pete! It could be anywhere. He probably buried it, planning to come back and dig it up."

"Yeah, that's what Danny thinks, too," Pete said.

31

"And maybe he was afraid he'd be caught," Mr. Whitney continued. "It would be much safer to bury it somewhere than carry it with him. Probably he buried it someplace away from the house. Maybe down by the river or off in the woods."

"So it really could be anywhere, like Danny said," Pete groaned.

"Cheer up, son. Let's take a look at the barn!"

Mr. Whitney unfastened the barn doors. They swung open with a creak. "I want to get an idea of what's in here," Mr. Whitney said. "Then some weekend we can start cleaning it out."

They peered into the dim interior. The barn had become a dumping ground for old tools and farm implements. Pete spotted a rusty plow, piles of old tires, and the remains of a Model T. He grinned at his father. "Hey, Dad, look at that! Think we could restore it?"

Mr. Whitney groaned. "You've got to be kidding. It would take forever."

"Just as long as I got to drive it," Pete joked. Then something else caught his eye. "Look, Dad — an old wagon."

"Take it easy," Mr. Whitney said, as Pete

scrambled over some old tires. "Remember what I said about snakes. Look before you step."

"Okay," Pete said. He worked his way across to the rear of the barn. "Wow! It's really old, Dad, but it sure is small. Is this the kind of wagon the settlers used?"

"Don't climb on it, Pete. The wood's probably rotten. It looks too small to be a Conestoga. Those wagons were big enough to carry an entire family, as well as all their belongings."

Pete pushed on the wood. Sure enough, some of it broke away, turning to powder in his hand.

"Okay, Pete, I think we've seen enough," his father said.

"Wait, Dad, I just want to see what's inside."

"There's not enough light. We'll check it out this weekend."

"Dad, there's stuff inside. Trunks and things." Then, when his father still hesitated, Pete added, "I bet Mom would never forgive us if this was full of antiques."

"Okay," Mr. Whitney sighed. "I'll go get a flashlight."

Pete grinned to himself. Then, because he couldn't wait for his father to return, he tugged at the handle of one of the old metal trunks. He had just managed to pry the trunk open, when his father joined him. His flashlight sent a strong beam of light over the contents.

"Oh, no," Pete groaned. "More junk."

"That'll teach you," Mr. Whitney grinned. "Well, let's see what we have here. Looks like old clothes and — " digging under piles of material " — candles, dishes, books. . . . Let's give up for today, okay, Pete?"

"Yeah." Pete was really disappointed. Those dumb Hatlers! Why did they have to save everything? It would take forever to sort through all this stuff.

Then, just as Mr. Whitney dropped the lid shut, Pete noticed something. "Dad, let me have the flashlight." He aimed the light at the top of the trunk. "Look, initials! Dad, this didn't belong to the Hatlers! S.D. Seth Delaney! This was Captain Scalawag's wagon!"

5

The following morning, Pete was able to persuade his mother to let him visit Danny. "But
stay out of the sun and don't play too hard," his
mother warned.

Play! Pete couldn't believe his mother's choice
of words. Playing was the last thing Pete had on
his mind. He had more important things to do —
namely, telling Danny that he'd found the captain's wagon in his barn! Danny might not think
they could find the treasure, but Pete was now
convinced it was possible. That wagon could eas-
ily be loaded with clues. Suddenly he was glad the
Hatlers had saved everything.

Unfortunately Danny wasn't alone. Duffy Snell
and several other boys were trying to organize a
baseball game in the field near Danny's house.

"Hey, Whitney, what are you doing tonight?" Duffy asked, when Pete joined the group.

"Nothing. Why?"

"Well, there's going to be a full moon and a bunch of us were thinking about going on a snipe hunt. You want to come?"

"A what?" Pete asked. Several of the boys tried to hide big grins, and a couple turned away, snickering. Pete had the uncomfortable feeling they were up to something funny.

"You never heard of snipe?" Duffy looked surprised. "Boy, you really are a flatlander!"

Pete flushed with anger. "Now, look here, Snell — "

"Whoa! Back off!" Duffy smiled innocently. "I didn't mean anything. Look, you really ought to come with us. Snipe hunts are real fun."

Pete tried to catch Danny's eye, but Danny just stared at his feet. "What are snipes?" Pete asked. "Some kind of fish?"

Duffy snorted. "Fish! Naw, they ain't fish. They're birds. Little brown birds that live down by the river. They come out at night to hunt for bugs. That's when we catch 'em."

"What do you do with them?" Pete, who'd never

gone hunting before, wished he could hide his ig-
norance.

"Nothing. After we catch 'em, we let 'em go.
There's nothing you can do with snipe."

"Why catch them?" Pete asked. It seemed like
a dumb thing to do.

"Well, it's like a contest. Just to see who can
catch the first one."

Pete scuffed the ground, considering.
"Well. . . ." It sounded boring, but Pete wanted
to fit in with the group. "Okay, I guess it'd be all
right."

"Great! We'll meet down by the swimming hole
about eight."

Pete hung around awhile longer, hoping to get
Danny off by himself, but Duffy stuck to Danny
like glue. The game got organized, and Pete saw
he wouldn't have a chance to talk to Danny alone.

On his way home, Pete tried to figure out what
Duffy was up to. He was sure that Duffy hadn't
forgotten their contest at the river. Duffy was the
kind of guy who'd lean on Pete till he felt he had
the upper hand. But the last thing Pete had expected was Duffy's friendliness today. He acted
like nothing had ever happened. And Danny had

been no help. There was something weird about this snipe hunt, but for the life of him Pete couldn't figure out what it could be. If Duffy planned on picking a fight tonight. . . . No, that didn't make sense. Well, even if he did, Pete wasn't worried. His judo training had taught him self-defense, even against someone Duffy's size.

Now Pete had to find a good excuse for going out that night. His mother still hadn't gotten used to the idea that he wouldn't be mugged the moment he set foot out the door after dark. His father was more understanding when Pete asked if he could go to Danny's house for the evening. "Sure. Just be back before ten, okay?"

"I don't know," Mrs. Whitney said. "That seems awfully late. Can't you boys get together tomorrow?"

While Pete was fumbling around for a reasonable excuse, Jessica burst into the kitchen. "Mom, help! Bob's picking me up in fifteen minutes! I'm not at all ready; I still have to dry my hair and my shirt needs to be ironed."

Pete sighed with relief. For once he was glad Jess had a date, even with a deputy sheriff.

Danny and Duffy were waiting by the big boulder with an armload of old gunnysacks. Duffy was acting impatient and Danny seemed uncomfortable. He barely looked at Pete.

"Took you long enough," Duffy grumbled. "We thought you'd never get here."

"Where are the others?" Pete asked suspiciously.

"Couldn't make it. Come on, let's quit wasting time. The moon's coming up."

The boys set off, following the river bank. The full moon painted the world black and silver. Any other time Pete would have enjoyed himself, but tonight he felt uneasy. Duffy had dropped the jovial, all-friends-together act and was back to his usual unpleasant self. And Danny was so tense, he reminded Pete of a coiled spring.

What was Duffy up to? Did he plan to dump him in the river? Lure him into the cave of some wild animal? Get him alone and pick a fight? That didn't make sense, either, because if there was one thing Pete was certain of, it was that Duffy needed an audience. Just having Danny there wasn't enough.

"How much farther?" Pete hissed.

"Quiet! You want to scare the snipe?"

Pete was quiet, but Duffy was making him mad. Finally, the boys broke through a small clump of pines and into the meadow beyond. Pete could smell the rank odor of wet vegetation. The only sound, besides crickets, was the noise of their sneakers squelching through the mud.

Suddenly Duffy stopped. "This is it."

"How do you know?" Pete whispered.

" 'Cause I do. Don't ask so many dumb questions." He thrust a gunnysack at Pete. "Now listen. Here's what you do," he whispered. "You get down low — no, dummy, down on your knees."

Pete lowered himself to the marshy patch of ground, feeling like an idiot. "Now what?"

"Now you take this sack and hold it open, like this. Then you make a noise, like this." Duffy demonstrated, making a squeaky sort of whistle. "Try it."

Pete wet his lips and tried to imitate the sound. Duffy snickered. "Not like that, like this." Pete listened, tried again, and finally mastered the sound.

"That's better," Duffy said. "You stay low, hold the bag open, make that sound, and wait."

"What for?

"Are you deaf? The snipe, what else?"

"But what do they do?"

"They'll hear you whistle and think it's another

snipe. They come looking and run right into the bag."

"Why would they do that?" Pete asked.

" 'Cause they're dumb." Pete could have sworn that he heard Duffy add "like you" under his breath.

"What'd you say?"

"Nothin'. You stay here. Me and Danny'll spread out. When you catch one, holler."

Duffy straightened up. "Okay, Danny, I'll go this way, you go over that way."

Danny was being very quiet. He took the gunnysack and started to squelch away into the darkness.

"Hey, Danny — " Pete called.

"Shut up!" Duffy protested. "You want to scare the snipe off?"

Duffy and Danny moved off in opposite directions and soon the darkness swallowed them. Mosquitoes rose out of the wet grass, and Pete felt some on his arms and neck. He slapped ineffectively. A frog croaked nearby, and Pete heard some crickets in the bushes. He wet his lips and tried the snipe whistle a few times, but nothing happened.

Time crawled by. Pete's legs began to cramp.

His muscles ached and his neck and arms itched from mosquito bites. He was beginning to feel drowsy. Suddenly he realized he hadn't heard either Duffy or Danny whistling. He leaned forward, straining to hear, but, except for the crickets and frogs, the silence was overwhelming.

Pete felt annoyed. He "halloed" a couple of times but got no answer. Surely they could hear him. Why didn't they answer?

Pete struggled to his feet. His jeans and sneakers were soaked with the smelly, foul mud he'd been kneeling in. He was tired and sore and bored to tears. What a rotten night this had turned out to be! Snipe or no snipe, he sure didn't want to hang around here any longer. He didn't care what Duffy thought of him; this was the last straw!

Pete picked up his gunnysack and started walking. In the darkness everything was shadowed and distorted, despite the full moon. Pete began to feel disoriented. It occurred to him that he couldn't hear the sound of the river. It should have been on his left, but when he stood still to listen, all he heard was a night wind sighing through the trees.

He began walking again, faster now, an uneasy feeling pricking at his skin. Once he tripped over a fallen log and fell. When he pulled himself up he was covered with sticky mud. He wiped his face with the rough, smelly gunnysack, cursing Duffy — and Danny, too.

Now Pete was beginning to feel afraid. He had no idea where he was. He knew that if you got lost, you were supposed to stay in one place until you were rescued. But he couldn't make himself stop walking.

Pete went faster and faster. He began to run. Trees reached out from nowhere to snatch at his hair and clothing. The uneven ground rose and fell sharply when he least expected it. Once he heard a sound that turned his blood to ice. Was it only a bird, or the cry of a wild animal prowling nearby?

The ground began to get steeper, gradually at first. Then Pete reached a sharp incline. He forced himself to stop, to catch his breath and explore the area in front of him. Blindly his hands touched what appeared to be the face of a cliff. Pete felt so discouraged he almost gave up. Then his shaking hands touched roots and clumps of weeds. He felt an indentation for a toehold here, a small projecting ledge of rock a bit higher. Pete began to climb.

There was no time to wonder how high he had

to go to reach the top. And he did not dare estimate how far he would fall if he missed his footing.

He shut his eyes, allowing his hands and feet to "see" each step ahead. Up and up, his heart beating madly, his arms and legs shaking with fear. He no longer gave a thought to Danny or Duffy. Suddenly the seemingly innocent snipe hunt had turned into a nightmare!

6

Pete's hand suddenly found level ground. He pulled himself over the edge of the embankment and rolled onto his back. For a long time he lay there, his heart pounding.

When he finally sat up, he saw the most welcome sight he could imagine. Headlights! The highway must be nearby.

By the time he'd scrambled across rough ground to the pavement, the car had passed by, but Pete wasn't worried. The familiar feeling of asphalt beneath his feet was reassuring. All he had to do was follow the highway until he found a house. Then he could phone his parents.

Another set of headlights, coming from behind like a searchlight,lit up the highway. Pete jumped up and down, waving his arms, to flag down the car.

The car slowed; the driver peered out. "What in the world — "

With a sinking feeling Pete realized he'd flagged down Bob Morris, Jessica's deputy sheriff.

"Hi," Pete said weakly.

"Pete? Pete Whitney?"

"Yes, sir. I'm Jessica's brother."

"I know who you are, but it's hard to recognize you under all that mud. What happened? Are you okay?"

"Yeah, I'm okay. It– it's kind of a long story. . . ."

"Get in the car and I'll take you home. Do your folks know where you are?"

"Uh, not exactly. They think I'm at a friend's house."

"And what were you really doing?"

Pete squirmed uncomfortably. "Well, uh, a bunch of the guys decided to go on a snipe hunt, so — "

"A snipe hunt!" Bob roared with laughter. "I should have guessed!"

Pete couldn't see what was so funny, but he had that same uneasy feeling he'd had earlier that he'd been fooled.

At last Bob was able to control himself. "Well,

Pete, I hate to tell you this, but you just got taken in by an old con."

"Oh, yeah?" Pete said, "How's that?"

"It's a joke, Pete. The local kids always pull it on a newcomer, especially someone from the city. I suppose they gave you a gunnysack and taught you the snipe whistle. Let's see if I can still do it." Bob made a whistling sound that was disgustingly familiar.

"Yeah," Pete muttered.

"Oh, that's great!" Bob chortled. "I didn't know anyone was pulling that off anymore."

Pete said nothing, but unconsciously he balled his hands into fists. He'd fallen right into Duffy's trap. Bob sensed Pete's anger. "Don't feel bad, Pete. The kids didn't mean to hurt you. They just wanted to have some fun. Where'd you go?"

"Down by the river," Pete said, trying to speak calmly.

"Who went with you?"

Pete remained silent, staring blindly out the window.

Bob sighed. "Okay, I understand. The thing is, you could have gotten hurt. You could have fallen in the river or really gotten lost."

Pete still said nothing.

"By now I guess you know they went home hours ago," Bob continued. "Look, Pete, I just want to explain things to them. They really meant no harm, but I want them to see how dangerous it was for them to just leave you out there."

"I can handle it," Pete said.

"Look, I know you're angry, but — "

Pete's temper snapped. "Angry!" he yelled. "Who, me? Naw, I'm not angry. I'm tired and filthy dirty and my folks'll probably have my head on a plate, but why should I be angry?"

"I know it's hard when you move to a new place," Bob said softly. "No friends, everything's different. But you'll catch on to our ways before you know it."

"Fat chance!" Pete slumped against the seat. "I hate this place."

They rode the rest of the way in silence, until Bob pulled up at the foot of Pete's driveway. As Pete started to climb out with a muttered "thanks," Bob put a hand on his shoulder. "Can I give you a piece of advice?"

Pete tensed. Every time he turned around someone wanted to give him advice.

"Try to meet these kids halfway," Bob said.

"Give them a chance. They aren't half bad, once you get to know them."

"Oh, sure," Pete sneered.

Bob sighed, pulling his hand away. "One of these days," he said, "some other city kid'll move here, and you'll probably be the first one to invite him on a snipe hunt!"

Pete looked at Bob in surprise and saw that he was grinning. "Thanks for the ride," Pete said coldly as he slammed the door shut. He heard a rattle of gravel as Bob pulled back to the highway.

Pete told his parents that Danny and he had gone frog hunting and he'd fallen in the mud. Before they could ask why he was home so late, he disappeared upstairs for a hot shower. When he reached his room, he fell across the bed and was asleep instantly.

He wasn't sure what woke him up. A distant rumble of voices seeped through his semi-conscious state. Company? At this hour? He rolled over to look at the luminous hands of his clock. His hand touched something warm and soft. A human hand! Someone lay on the bed next to him.

His eyes, becoming accustomed to the dark room, made out the form of a small child.

The whole room had changed. His bed was covered with a quilt instead of his blue spread. The furniture was different and the curtains at the window were lace, not cotton. There was no clock.

Pete slipped off the bed, discovering an unfamiliar woven rug covering the wooden floor. He tiptoed to the window and peered outside.

Where the hills rose gently behind the house, there now stood a full-grown orchard. Near the barn, which looked newly painted, were pens and corrals. Pete could hear the soft movement of animals.

He crossed to the door and slipped into the hall. No nightlight glowed. He moved on to his parents' room, where he found other children lying asleep on a strange bed.

Suddenly Pete realized he was dressed in unfamiliar clothing, not the favorite ragged pajamas he'd put on earlier. He stared down at his feet and saw a dirty piece of bandage wrapped around the big toe, but he didn't remember hurting his foot. An old-fashioned clock chimed downstairs. I'm dreaming, he thought. He shut his eyes and counted to ten. When he opened them, he was still in the same dream.

It was happening again! Pete rubbed his face, but it didn't feel like his face at all! Not even his face was his own. He crept down the hall to the bathroom to look in the mirror. But when he opened the bathroom door, he found himself staring into a linen closet scented with dried lavender. Where was the bathroom?

He leaned weakly against the wall, fighting back an urge to panic! He had to think things out. First, this was no dream! Pete was in someone else's body and in some other time. The realization was so horrifying he didn't really want to believe it.

He tiptoed to the head of the stairs, listening. Voices drifted up to him, but he couldn't make out the words. Slowly he eased himself down the stairs, careful to make no noise. At the bottom he squatted under the banister, straining to hear what was being said.

"Y'all must remember, the best way to help your kin is with gold. Yankee dollars will buy food, clothin', and medicines." The voice, in a heavy Southern drawl, was powerful without being loud.

"But Cap'n, we aren't rich. We're just farmers. Last year me and my missus lost nearly all our crops to late frost. We had to borrow at the bank to get us through the year. Our place is mortgaged to the hilt. Ain't no way we can borrow more. So how are we goin' to give when we ain't got nothin' to give?"

"Now, Hiram, that ain't so," a woman's voice protested. "Here, Cap'n Delaney. You take this brooch of mine. It belonged to my grandmother. She was born and raised in Georgia. I figure she'd like to know it was going for a worthy cause, to feed her kin."

"Sarah, what do you want to go and do a fool thing like that for? That little brooch ain't worth nothin'."

"Hiram, that's not so," the captain said. "These little seed pearls may not look like much, but they're set in gold and they'll fetch something. Your grandmother would be proud of you, Sarah Owens. I know this is a sacrifice, but you have to look into your hearts, folks. Hiram, you and your missus have food on the table and a roof over your heads. I'm here to tell you there are folks back home who don't even have that!"

There was a buzz of conversation. Captain Scalawag! Pete could hardly believe he was actually overhearing the captain as he worked his con! Man, what a line! Pete was beginning to feel weak, but he still didn't want to miss anything the captain said.

"Now I have a question." A different man spoke. "I'm wondering just how you propose to get this money to the South. That's a long journey, Cap'n, and I don't think the Yanks will take kindly to us just sashaying through their lines to help their enemy."

"You're right about that, John. But I have a plan to smuggle that treasure right through enemy lines, if need be. Right under the noses of those Yankee devils!"

Suddenly, Pete felt a wave of nausea and his head spun madly. He clung tightly to the banister, but he must have groaned, for a woman suddenly appeared in the doorway.

"Zeb, you rascal, what are you doing up?"

She was a plump woman, with a flushed face and dark hair screwed into a knot at the nape of her neck. Her long skirts swept the floor.

Pete tried to pull himself to his feet, but he

was too dizzy. He swayed, clutching at the banister.

"Zeb!" She hurried to the foot of the stairs. "You're ill, child!"

A moment later, another woman joined her. "Zeb Tyler, have you been eavesdropping?" the woman said. Pete recognized her from the general store — it was Mrs. Tyler! Mrs. Tyler took one look at him and put her hand on his forehead. "Oh, you're burning up, son!"

"He does seem to feel poorly," the plump woman agreed. "I hope he isn't coming down with the ague. Zeb, you and Willy been playing down in the river bottom again? You boys know that air is poison!"

"Oh, Lena," Mrs. Tyler said with a gasp, "they've got the cholera over to Hangtown. You don't suppose. . . ." Her frightened voice trailed away as the two women exchanged worried glances.

As sick as Pete was, the name clicked in his mind. Lena? *Lena Hatler?* But of course! This was her house!

"Now don't fret, Lavinia," Lena Hatler said grimly. "No use worrying till we're sure. I'll just brew up a cup of camomile tea for the boy. That'll sweat the fever right out of him. Take him upstairs and. . . ."

Her voice faded; her face started to blur. Pete blinked, feeling himself begin to sway. Strong arms reached out to catch him as he fell into darkness.

7

When Pete woke up again, the sun was shining, and he heard the sound of the lawn mower next door. He sat up, nearly laughing aloud with relief! He was in his own room with its familiar furniture, bedspread, and curtains.

Pete looked at his feet. No bandage. He touched his face. It was his own!

Could it have been a dream after all? It had seemed so real, right down to the scent of lavender and the feel of rough boards beneath his bare feet. But how could he find out? Maybe there was a clue in those old journals.

He dressed quickly and went downstairs. Everybody had eaten breakfast earlier. His father must have gone to work, and Jessica was probably out horseback riding. Pete gulped down toast and a glass of milk and went looking for his mother. He found her in the attic.

"Hi, Pete. Sleep well?"

"Uh, yeah, okay. Mom, can I borrow those journals you were reading?"

Mrs. Whitney stared at her son in surprise. "I guess so. Why?"

"Well. . . ." He fished around for an excuse. "I'm still curious about that treasure."

She grinned. "Ah, the lure of buried gold! All right, but you have to take good care of them. Oh, by the way, I also found some photo albums, and there's one picture I want you to see." Carefully she opened an album to a picture of the Hatler house. "See? There's the apple orchard."

"Wow! When was this taken?" Pete studied the brown and white photograph.

"It says on the back, *1904*. See the man standing by the fence? That was Lena Hatler's son, Tom."

"Wow!" Pete said again. It was incredible! The house, the barn, the orchard! This picture looked very much like what he'd seen last night. "Mom, are there any other pictures?"

"There are several albums," Mrs. Whitney said. "Where do you want to start?"

"Did you find a picture of Captain Scalawag?"

"Sorry, Pete, I'm afraid I can't help you there."

Pete was disappointed. "What about Zeb Tyler?"

"No, this is just the Hatler family. In Zeb's time, people didn't usually have cameras of their own, unless they were photographers. So having your picture taken was kind of special."

Pete had struck out again. Absentmindedly he thumbed back through the album. It was interesting to see the old pictures, but after a few pages, Pete grew bored. He turned the pages faster, barely glancing at the faces.

And then his hand froze in midair. Quickly he whipped a page back.

"Be careful!" his mother squealed. "That book is fragile."

Pete barely heard her. He was staring at the picture of a woman holding a small boy.

"Who's this, Mom?"

"Let me look. Maybe there's some identification on the back." Mrs. Whitney gingerly pried the old photo from the page. Turning it over, she read, " *Lena Elizabeth Hatler and Thomas Edward Hatler, age 7.*' Pete, remember what Mrs. Hatler wrote in her journal, about the Civil War being fought by young boys, and her son was almost seven? This picture must have been taken about the time Captain Scalawag was working for her."

Pete didn't need any reminders. He was staring at the photo. This was the face of the woman who, just hours — or a century — ago had offered to make tea for a boy with a fever! Remembering the fever reminded him of something else. "Mom, what's 'ague'?"

"Ague? Pete, you ask the strangest questions! Let me think. As I recall, it was an old-fashioned term for malaria. But where did you hear that word? It's never used anymore."

"I must have heard it on TV." The excuse sounded a little lame, even to Pete. "Thanks, Mom. I have to go."

"But I thought you wanted to read those journals!"

"I'll look at them later." He took the stairs two at a time and ran out of the house.

Pete had to think. And he knew that the best way to clear his head would be to take a long walk. There had to be some explanation for these strange things that were happening to him.

He walked along the road toward town. One thing was certain. These "dreams" were definitely not dreams. The picture of Mrs. Hatler had proved that once and for all. So, what was happening?

Incredible as it seemed, Pete knew it had something to do with traveling through time. But his body wasn't traveling, only his mind. He remembered a weird "truth-is-stranger-than-fiction" show on TV about people who claimed to be able to leave their bodies. They called it "astral projection." The idea of leaving his own body and traveling back into a previous century gave Pete the creeps. He shivered, although the sun was hot.

Worse yet, he apparently had no control over these events. One minute he was himself, and the next minute he was Zeb Tyler!

But *why* was it happening? As far as he knew, he didn't have ESP.

Then Pete had a crazy idea. No, it was too weird to even consider. It even gave him the shudders. And yet. . . .

What if Zeb Tyler was calling to him from beyond the grave? What if Zeb somehow knew of Pete's fascination with the treasure and was causing all this to happen, to have Pete experience what Zeb had experienced, to give Pete some kind of message?

Pete shook his head. How could his experience in the general store be important? Unless . . . maybe Zeb hadn't quite mastered "astral projection" at that time. Maybe it was an experiment of sorts. But last night he had stayed in Zeb's body for a longer period of time. He'd even heard the captain speak. Maybe Zeb was getting the hang of it, after all.

Then Pete thought of something so terrible he stopped dead in his tracks. Each time he'd been in Zeb's body, he'd felt ill. Zeb had died of cholera, soon after the Fourth of July celebration. What if Pete got trapped in Zeb's body and couldn't get back to his own time before Zeb died? *Would Pete die with Zeb?* The idea was just too frightening. One thing was obvious: The lost treasure, the captain, and Zeb were somehow connected. And it was up to Pete to find out how.

"Maybe that's it!" Pete said aloud. "Maybe Zeb figured out where the captain hid the treasure, but he died before he could tell anyone!"

Pete had been concentrating so hard, he was surprised to find he'd walked all the way to Main Street. He spotted Danny and a couple of the other kids across the street.

Seeing Danny reminded Pete of the snipe hunt,

61

and he felt a fresh surge of anger. Darn it all, Danny was supposed to be his friend! How come he'd gone along with Duffy and hadn't warned Pete?

"Hey, Danny, I want to talk to you," Pete yelled.

Danny's expression, when he saw Pete, wasn't what Pete had expected. "What are you doing here?" Danny demanded.

"Now, look — " Pete began, but Danny interrupted him.

"Duffy's looking for you, Pete, and boy, is he mad! If he catches you, he's going to tear you apart. You'd better stay out of sight for a few days, at least until he calms down."

"Wait a minute!" Pete said. "I'm the one who's mad! You guys left me down there by the river. Some friend you turned out to be!"

"Look, I'm sorry," Danny said, but he sounded more worried than sorry. "It was a joke, that's all."

"Oh, it was funny, all right. Absolutely hilarious."

"I said I was sorry!" Danny snapped.

"I can see that. Boy, I can tell you're really sorry. Listen, how come you didn't warn me, huh? How come?"

"Duffy would have killed me," Danny said miserably. "I know you won't believe this, but I didn't want to leave you there. Honest, Pete."

"Wait a minute. If this whole thing was Duffy's idea, how come he's mad at me now?"

"Because this morning Deputy Morris was asking some of the kids about the snipe hunt. Duffy figures you snitched."

"Are you guys crazy? I wouldn't do that. Bob picked me up last night on the highway and gave me a ride home. When he asked me what I was doing out there in the middle of the night, what could I say? I told him about the snipe hunt, but I never said who I was with. Never!"

"Duffy thinks you did," Danny said. "He's out to get you."

"He's been out to get me ever since we met!" Pete said angrily. "What'd I ever do to him?"

"It's not you, Pete." Danny looked uncomfortable. "Duffy always picks on new kids. It makes him feel important. He's hard-headed and a real bully. And once he gets his mind on something, he won't back down. One way or another, you're going to have to fight him. He's bigger than you, Pete, a lot bigger. And I know he won't fight fair."

8

Pete didn't know what to do. The last thing he wanted was a fight with Duffy. But at the same time, he couldn't just go and hide.

"Well, what are you waiting for?" Danny demanded. "If Duffy catches you. . . ."

"Danny, I can't worry about Duffy right now. I have to find out more about Zeb Tyler and that treasure. It may be a matter of life or death!"

Danny sighed. "You really won't give up on this, will you? Well, I've told you everything I know."

"Isn't there anyone in town who knows about it?" Pete asked. "What about that doctor who took care of me the day I fainted? He seemed to know a lot about the old days."

Danny snapped his fingers. "Pete! I just thought of something. There's an old man in town, lived here all his life — his father actually *knew* the captain. Sure . . . you should talk to him — Old Packy Coates."

Coates. The name sounded familiar to Pete, but he couldn't place it.

"Where does he live?" Pete asked.

"Come on, I'll show you."

Danny led the way down several side streets, finally stopping before a small white cottage with a front garden filled with flowers. A white picket fence surrounded the house and garden. An old man was sitting in a rocking chair on the wide front porch.

"Hi, Mr. Coates," Danny yelled. Then, in a low voice, he added, "He's kind of hard of hearing."

"Hi, there, Danny. Come on up and sit awhile. Who's your friend?"

"This is Pete Whitney," Danny said, pushing open the gate. The boys joined the old man on the front porch. Danny made the introductions a second time so Packy Coates could hear them. Packy had to be at least ninety, maybe close to a hundred years old. He looked like a wrinkled old tortoise, except for his blue eyes, which snapped and sparkled. He grinned a toothless grin at Pete. "Hatler house, huh? My pa used to play around the Hatler place when he was a boy. Matter of fact, he 'n' his buddy, Zeb Tyler, used to steal Widow Hatler's apples." The old man cackled. "Made her madder 'n' a wet hen. She used to chase the boys with her broom. Never caught 'em, though."

Now Pete remembered where he'd heard the name Coates before. Mrs. Hatler had written about Willy Coates in her journal. Packy's father must have been Willy Coates, Zeb's friend and partner-in-crime in the apple orchard. Pete felt a shiver of excitement. "Your father also knew Captain Scalawag, didn't he?" Pete prompted.

"Oh sure. Everyone knew the captain. What a scoundrel he was! Smooth-talkin' and good-lookin'. Guess you heard about the treasure."

"Yes, sir."

"Reminds me of the day he was hanged. My pa saw him strung up!"

Pete and Danny gasped. "He did?" they said together.

"Yes sir! Fact is, it was Zeb who caught the captain trying to sneak out of town."

"Zeb Tyler. But how — "

"Way my pa told it, Zeb was sick with a fever. His ma gave him strict orders to stay in bed on that Fourth of July. But you know how kids are. Zeb got to feelin' better and couldn't stand to miss the celebration. So he climbed out the back window and cut across the fields, through Mrs. Hatler's place. That's when he spotted the captain, hitching up his wagon like he was clearing out. The captain had hitched up the widow's horse along with his own. That rascal was not only takin' the treasure, he was stealin' her favorite mare!"

The old man paused. "Then what happened?" Pete prompted.

"When Zeb realized what the captain was up to, he hightailed it into town to warn the folks. Then he passed out. A bunch of the men rode out to the Hatler place and, sure enough, they caught the captain on one of the back roads. They brought him back to Oak Bluff, and the sheriff put him in jail. The folks searched his wagon, but they couldn't find the treasure. They couldn't make that devil tell 'em where it was, so they took him out of jail, put him up on a horse, and started to string him up from a tree. They only meant to scare him, you understand, but his horse bolted and before they could cut him down, he was dead!"

Pete shivered. "Then what happened?"

"Well, that calmed folks down some. Most of 'em went on home, probably feeling a mite ashamed. But some of 'em went out to the Hatler place and started to tear it up, lookin' for that treasure. They dug up her garden, but they never found it."

"What do you think the captain did with it?" Pete asked.

Packy Coates shrugged. "Hard to say. He could've buried it somewheres or hidden it somewheres else. No one ever knew for sure. There's a lot of places that treasure could be."

"But if Zeb saw the captain," Pete said, "didn't he see what the captain did with the treasure?"

"Like I said, the boy passed out after all that running. He never got better. Fever just got worse, and he kept hallucinatin' about the captain. I don't think he ever did see that treasure 'cause all he talked about was the widow's horse. And then he died a week later. Almost killed his ma, it did."

The old man leaned back in his chair and closed his eyes. "Yes sir, like . . . to . . . have. . . ." His mumbling gave way to a gentle snore.

"He's asleep," Danny whispered. Pete nodded and the two boys tiptoed down the front walk. Once outside the picket fence, Pete broke into a run.

"Hey, wait up!" Danny hollered. "Where're you going now?"

"Home!" Pete called over his shoulder. "I've got an idea about that treasure."

"What?" Danny panted, trying to keep up.

"Just an idea. I forgot to tell you, I found the captain's wagon in our barn."

"So what? Everyone knows that!"

"They do?" Pete slowed to a walk, looking disappointed.

"Pete, how many times do we have to tell you! The wagon was searched!"

"But there must be something there," Pete said. "Why would the captain leave the treasure behind? It has to be in that wagon!"

"Why won't you believe us? He buried it because he wanted to come back later to dig it up. Did you look in the wagon?"

"Yeah, it's full of junk."

"I told you so!"

"I know, but — "

"You better stop thinking about that treasure and figure out what you're going to do about Duffy."

Pete groaned. "I'd like to forget about him."

"Well, you can't. I figure in a few days he'll calm down. Of course you might miss the Fourth of July celebration, but — "

"Hold on!" Pete stopped so suddenly, Danny almost tripped over him. "Do you think I'm scared of Duffy? Look, I don't want to have to fight him, but I'm not going to run from him, either."

"But Pete — "

"Forget it, Danny. If I back out, he'll never let me live it down. Sooner or later, I've got to face him!"

Pete began walking again, faster this time, with Danny scrambling to keep up. They rounded the last curve in the road so suddenly that Pete almost collided with Duffy, who was coming from the opposite direction. When Pete recovered his balance, he looked straight into Duffy's angry face. Duffy stood in the middle of the road, hands on hips, feet wide apart, blocking Pete's path.

"I've been looking for you," Duffy snarled. "You told Deputy Morris about the snipe hunt. You trying to get me in trouble?"

"I didn't tell anyone," Pete said. "Bob Morris picked me up on the road last night. Yeah, I told him I'd been on a snipe hunt, but I never said who with. If Bob was asking questions, he's only guessing."

"Oh, yeah? Well, I say you're a liar!"

Pete counted silently to five. He would have loved to smash his fist into Duffy's fat, red face, but he knew that was exactly what Duffy wanted.

"What's the matter, flatlander, can't you talk?" Duffy sneered.

"Forget it!" Pete said. "I'm not going to fight you."

"Oooh, the little city boy doesn't want to get his pretty white hands dirty," Duffy protested mockingly.

"Leave me alone, Snell!"

"Oooh, oooh, I'm scared to death," Duffy taunted.

Pete studied Duffy silently, taking his time. Duffy was doing everything he could to make sure Pete threw the first punch. Pete had had enough judo to know that would be his downfall. He also knew there was no way to avoid a fight. But as long as Pete kept calm, he had the upper hand. Duffy was several inches taller and he outweighed Pete, but that didn't mean he would win.

"Okay," Pete said quietly. "You want to fight? That's fine with me. But not here."

"Oh, brother!" Duffy spat into the dust at Pete's feet. "Quit stalling, Whitney."

"We'll go to my place," Pete said. "It's close. There's a big field out behind the barn. No one will see us."

Duffy nodded. "Suits me! Let's go!"

Pete pushed past Duffy and started walking. Behind him he heard Duffy chuckle.

9

There was a lot of junk lying behind the old barn: scrap lumber, piles of rock, even some rusting metal.

"Let's go out to the field," Pete said. "We'll have more room."

"Huh-uh!" Duffy shook his head. "This is fine with me. We've got plenty of room."

Pete could guess what was going on in Duffy's mind. There were plenty of rough two-by-fours on the lumber pile, and Duffy kept looking at them. He did not intend to lose!

"Well, let's get it over with," Duffy snarled. He planted his feet wide apart, crouching slightly, like a Japanese sumo wrestler, his beefy arms extended as if to hug Pete. "Come on!" he roared.

"You want me, come and get me." Pete laughed.

Duffy lowered his head like a bull and charged.

Pete stood his ground until the last second, when he lightly stepped aside. Caught off balance, Duffy sprawled on his face. He struggled to his feet, looking startled. There was an ugly scrape across one cheek, and he touched it and winced. For a moment he glared at Pete. Then, with a snarl, he charged again.

This time he hit his mark! Pete rolled backward, letting his body relax and go with the roll, his hands grasping Duffy's forearms, his feet under Duffy's stomach. Suddenly Pete's feet shot out and Duffy flew over Pete's head, landing on his face a second time.

Pete was on his feet in an instant, ready for the next attack. This time it took Duffy longer to get up. The breath had been knocked from him. He made it to his hands and knees, shaking his head slowly from side to side as if to clear his vision. He roared with pain and anger, and Pete was reminded of a wild animal. This was no longer a challenge. Duffy would keep fighting until he dropped or smashed Pete to pieces. And if Pete won this round, Duffy would find another opportunity to get even. And next time he'd give Pete no warning!

Pete felt his stomach knot with fear, but fear was his worst enemy. He forced himself to breathe slowly and deeply, to stay calm and look Duffy straight in the eye.

"Come on, Snell, let's call it quits." He extended a hand in Duffy's direction, his eyes never leaving Duffy's face.

Duffy's answer was a snarl of rage. He struggled to his feet, weaving slightly.

"I don't want to fight you anymore," Pete said. "Let's call it a draw, okay?"

He had barely finished the sentence when Duffy charged again. Pete stepped quickly aside, catching Duffy's arm and flipping him over. Duffy landed on his back with a loud thud. For a moment Duffy lay in the dirt, his eyes closed, his chest heaving.

"You knocked him out!" Danny said in amazement.

Pete shook his head. "No. He just had the wind knocked out him."

Pete stepped forward to help Duffy to his feet, but at the last moment, Duffy opened his eyes and Pete quickly drew back. Duffy's eyes glittered with fury. He rolled to his stomach, groaning.

Slowly he pulled himself to his hands and knees, then to his feet. He staggered, caught his balance, and moved away from Pete.

For an instant Pete's hopes rose. Maybe Duffy had had enough. Then Duffy lunged at the lumber pile, and when he turned to face Pete, he was grinning maliciously. In one great fist he held a big piece of rough wood.

"No!" Danny shouted, stepping forward, as if to stop Duffy.

"Danny, get back!" Pete yelled. "Keep out of his way."

"That's not fair!" Danny said. "Put it down, Duffy!"

Duffy swung his club at Danny with a snarl. Danny ducked and the wood sliced the air, making a whizzing sound.

"Danny, get out of here!" Pete yelled frantically. He knew that Duffy would smash anything or anyone in his path. Pete felt fairly certain he could handle Duffy as long as he didn't have to worry about Danny, too.

Suddenly Pete was distracted by a movement at the base of the lumber pile. He turned to look, gasped, and froze. A large snake, which had probably been sleeping underneath the sun-warmed lumber, had been rudely awakened when Duffy grabbed the wood. Pete had never seen a real live rattlesnake before, but he knew without a doubt this was one! As he watched, nearly hypnotized with fear, the snake began crawling out of the woodpile, its black tongue forking in and out like lightning. In a moment it would reach Duffy's leg.

"Duffy!" Pete yelled. "Snake! Look!"

But Duffy neither moved nor looked. "Nice try, but it won't work," he snarled.

Danny, seeing the snake, yelled, too, but Duffy just grinned. Nothing was going to stop him! Pete had no time to think or yell another warning. He made a swift dive at Duffy, the force of his movement sending them both flying away from the lumber pile. Pete's head struck the wall of the barn. He felt an intense rush of pain, then everything went black.

When Pete regained consciousness, he was alone. The first thing he noticed was the sound of someone whistling inside the barn. Slowly Pete sat up, shaking his head to clear the fuzziness. Where was everyone? Had Pete and Danny gone for help?

He looked around and gasped. Everything had

changed. Gone were the piles of lumber, rocks, and scrap metal. No longer was the field a weedy, unused patch of ground. Tall, green stalks of corn rose before him in long, neat rows. Somewhere a cow bawled and chickens cackled.

Pete's head ached and he reached up to rub it. A battered felt hat fell to his feet. Pete shuddered. He looked down at his clothes. Different. He was barefoot and there was that dirty scrap of bandage around his toe! *It* was happening again!

He got slowly to his feet, feeling dizzy. The whistling inside caught his attention again. He looked at the newly painted wood, spotting a hole lower in the wall. He knelt down and put his eye to the hole.

At first he couldn't see anything. As he became accustomed to the dim lighting, the first thing he was able to make out was a man sitting on a wagon. Around him were several opened trunks filled with an assortment of things: sewing notions, kettles, sadirons, clothing, material, even a trunkful of books.

While Pete watched, the man finished packing the trunks, fastened them shut, and, with a great deal of difficulty, lifted them into the wagon. Then, still whistling, he led a horse from its stall.

Pete winced as a fresh wave of dizziness washed over him. His head was pounding now and his legs felt weak. He slid back down to a sitting position, resting his head against the hot boards of the barn wall. The world was swimming in a shimmery haze. Familiar blackness engulfed him and he closed his eyes.

But when he opened them, nothing had changed. The man in the barn was still whistling. A bird perched nearby on a fence post looked curiously at Pete. Bees hummed in the hot stillness. He had not made the journey back, after all. All of a sudden, Pete felt trapped in time!

Slowly he pushed himself to his feet. He had to get to Oak Bluff right away. He had to tell the others. . . .

What others? Pete shook his head, trying to clear his thoughts. He had to get back to the house, lie down. . . .

Get to town, tell the folks. . . .

Suddenly Pete realized that his mind and Zeb's were intermingling. Pete had been in Zeb's body longer than ever before, and Zeb was trying to do what'd he'd done a century before — get to town to warn the people that the captain was going to escape with their treasure.

Pete shivered, partly from the fever, partly from fear. What he had been dreading was coming true. He was trapped in Zeb's body! He had to get loose, to get back to his own body and his own time.

The desire to warn the people grew stronger. Zeb was taking control. Pete had to do something fast. He knew that if he gave in to Zeb, he was lost. If Zeb wanted to go to town, Pete would do just the opposite. He would try to get back to the house where, in his own time, his mother was working in the attic.

Slowly Pete forced himself onto his hands and knees. He tried to stand up but he hadn't the strength. At last he gave up trying to get to his feet and began to crawl along beside the back wall of the barn. Hot gravel bit into his palms. The sun beat down on his head and back. Perspiration rolled off his forehead into his eyes, blurring his vision. The smell of dust rose to his nostrils, choking him. Pete reached the corner of the barn with tremendous effort.

"Pete!"

He stopped! Someone had called his name. He shook his head, trying again to clear the fuzziness. But there was no one there.

The captain began singing a jovial tune in a deep bass from inside the barn. Pete heard the rattle of a harness and the soft clopping of horses' hooves. "Easy, Rosie. Whoa, babe!" The captain led the team and wagon out of the barn, into the yard.

"Pete!"

He heard his name again, over the captain's voice.

Someone was calling to him from the twentieth century. Maybe his idea was working! All he had to do was keep crawling away from the direction Zeb wanted him to go. But if the captain saw Zeb. . . .

The team and wagon came into view, the captain walking at the horses' heads. "Whoa, girl!" The horses stopped. They whinnied softly.

"Two horses!" The words broke from Pete's lips like a small explosion. Two horses? He hadn't even thought about horses, so why — Zeb again! Zeb's mind, Zeb's surprise. But what did two horses have to do with his predicament?

Pete had a hazy memory of Zeb's concern over the Widow Hatler's stolen horse. But before he could wonder why, the captain turned. He had heard Zeb's voice! For a split second he frowned, as if puzzled. Then, "Zeb Tyler? What in tarnation? . . ."

"Pete!"

Got to get to town, have to tell the others . . . *two* horses. Pete groaned. The captain was coming toward him; Pete felt Zeb's panic. Pete was so close to his own time and yet so far away. In a week Zeb would be dead! If Pete didn't break loose *now*, he'd die, too!

10

"Let me go," Pete moaned. "Please, Zeb, let me go back."

"Zeb, what's the matter with you, boy?" The captain was coming closer and closer.

"Please," Pete begged. "If you don't let me go, you'll never get to town in time. He'll catch you! The captain will stop you. . . ."

"Pete!" The voice broke through again.

The captain moved on, walking through a haze of shimmery light. The world tilted at an angle and began to spin, like a carnival ride. Pete was drawn down into a dark whirlpool. Down he spun, faster and faster, until there was nothing but blackness. And silence.

Voices. Far way. Coming closer, closer. . . .

The dizziness receded, darkness turned slowly to light. Pete opened his eyes.

"Pete, get up!"

Pete blinked, the hot sun blinding him. "Danny?" He squinted, shading his eyes with his hand. Danny's face swam into focus.

"You okay?" Danny asked.

"I — I think so. What happened?"

"Don't you remember? You and Duffy were fighting and — "

Duffy! Pete struggled to sit up, and saw Duffy squatting near the woodpile, watching him closely. "Whitney, you okay?" Duffy asked.

"Yeah. . . ." Pete rubbed his head, wincing when his hand felt a lump. "I guess I hit my head." Suddenly his hand froze. At Duffy's feet lay the mangled remains of the snake. "The snake! Now I remember. It was coming for you, Duffy."

"Yeah," Duffy said. "You pushed me out of the way just in time." He scowled and for an instant Pete thought he was angry. Then, without looking at Pete, Duffy said, "I guess you saved my life, Whitney."

Pete didn't know what to say. Finally, in a gruff voice, he asked, "Did you kill it?"

"Yeah. He tried to crawl away but I got him with that piece of wood." Duffy grinned. "He's a big sucker." He picked the snake up by the rattles.

Pete stared at the snake in awe. "Weren't you scared he'd strike?"

"You gotta know how to kill it," Duffy said. "Maybe I'll show you sometime."

Pete grinned. "Thanks. I'd like that."

"Tell you what," Duffy said offhandedly. "I'll show you how to take care of snakes if you show me some of that stuff you did when we were fighting. You know. . . ." He didn't need to go on. Pete understood

"That's judo," Pete said. "Yeah, I can show you a few things."

Duffy was silent, but he looked pleased. Pete knew that there would be no more trouble between them.

"Hey, what're you going to do with the snake?" Danny asked. "You going to show it to your mom, Pete?"

"You crazy? She'd pass out!" They all laughed. "Hey, wait a minute," Pete said. "I've got an idea. Let me get my camera and take a picture of it.

The guys in the city never saw a snake that big!"

Pete got to his feet too fast. For a moment he felt unsteady. "You okay?" Danny said.

"Yeah, I'm okay. Just don't tell my mom. If she knew I was knocked out, she'd put me in the hospital."

"You weren't knocked out," Danny said. "You just had the wind knocked out of you."

"Are you sure?" Pete asked with a frown.

"Sure I'm sure. You hit your head, but you weren't knocked out. You kept groaning and talking, so I knew you weren't out."

"What'd I say?"

"Oh, I don't know. Something crazy about horses."

Horses! That reminded Pete of Zeb and the captain. The memory of the time he'd spent in Zeb's body was so real, Pete was sure he'd been unconscious for an hour or more. Thinking of Zeb made Pete feel anxious about something. But what was it?

"Go get your camera," Danny said. "We'll wait here. We don't want to scare your mom."

"Right," Pete said absentmindedly, his mind still on Zeb and the captain. He walked slowly back to the house, in a daze. It was still so vivid — the captain, the wagon, the horses. . . .

Once in his room, Pete tried to find his camera. What a mess his room was. It didn't usually bother him until, like now, he was looking for something.

His mother appeared in the doorway. "What in the world are you doing?" she asked.

"I'm looking for my camera," Pete said, tossing a pile of clothes — clean and dirty — together into a heap on the bed. "I can't find it."

"Are you sure you unpacked it?" She began sorting through the clothes, her nose wrinkling at the mess Pete was making.

"I took it out of the camera bag, but I don't know where I put it."

"Stop throwing things around! You're just making things worse. Did you look in the closet?"

"Mom, I wouldn't put it in the closet," Pete said impatiently. "It's supposed to be on my chest of drawers."

Mrs. Whitney moved to her son's side. After a moment she tapped him on the shoulder. "What?" he barked.

"Look! It's on top of your chest of drawers, right under your nose!"

Pete stopped pawing through a drawer and stared at all the things on top of his dresser. Suddenly he spotted the camera, still neatly packed in a small brown case.

"I must have looked right at it," he cried, grabbing it.

"You aren't used to seeing it in its case, Pete," Mrs. Whitney laughed. "I've done that lots of times myself — looked for something that was right under my nose, because I expected to see it differently."

Pete, halfway to the door, froze in his tracks. "What did you say?" He turned suddenly to stare at her.

"I said — Pete, what's wrong!"

"That's it!" Pete yelled. "The treasure! I know where it is!"

"What?"

"Come on!" He raced down the stairs, his mother close on his heels. Halfway across the yard he yelled to Danny and Duffy.

"Pete, what are you doing?" Mrs. Whitney cried, watching her son as if he'd gone crazy. Pete didn't answer. He was tugging at the barn doors. Duffy and Danny came around the corner of the barn.

"The treasure!" Pete said quickly. "I figured it out. It's in the barn."

"Pete, are you — "

"Don't talk, Danny, just help me get these doors open."

The barn doors opened with a squeaking of unoiled hinges. They were met with a blast of hot, musty air. Pete began to move the junk that blocked his path.

"Maybe we should wait for your father — " Mrs. Whitney began.

"Come on!" Pete said impatiently. "Help me clear a path to the wagon."

"Oh Pete. There you go again!" Danny said. "How many times do I have to tell you that the wagon was searched?"

Pete stopped and turned to face the others. "That's right," he said, "the wagon was searched, but the treasure was right there. The people looked right at it, but they never saw it."

"That's impossible!" Duffy snorted. "You can't look at something and not see it!"

"Oh, yes you can," Pete grinned. "I just did, didn't I, Mom? I looked right at my camera and never saw it, because I didn't expect to see it in its case."

"Pete, if this is just a wild guess — " Mrs. Whitney began.

"If it is, I'll clean everything up afterward. I promise. Come on, isn't it worth a try?"

Mrs. Whitney, Duffy, and Danny exchanged looks. Then, "Oh, heck, let's do it!" Duffy said, putting his shoulder to an old barrel. He pushed it aside to widen the path to the wagon. It was all the incentive the others needed.

In about twenty minutes, the four had cleared a wide path to the back of the barn where the wagon stood. "The wood is rotten," Pete warned, "so we can't climb on it. Let's unload the wagon and take all the stuff out to the yard where we can see what we're doing."

"The wagon's full of trunks," Danny said. "You said you looked inside already."

"I did," Pete grinned. "They're full of junk. The kind of stuff a peddler would have."

"I hope you know what you're doing," Danny grumbled. "It's too darn hot to do all this work for nothing."

Together they carried the trunks into the yard, and Pete opened them all. Even though he knew what they contained, it was a bit of a shock to see the same items in the trunk that he'd just watched the captain packing — in another time!

Mrs. Whitney reached into one trunk and scooped out an armful of rich, violet-colored taffeta. "Look at this!" She shook out the material. "Good heavens, there must be twenty yards of material in this dress. But how hideous! Beadwork, fringe. . . ." She giggled, holding it up against herself. "It's in remarkable condition, though. Still, who would want to wear it?"

"What's this?" Danny asked, pulling out a collection of small metal cans. He peered at the label. "Dr. Pur — Pur — "

Mrs. Whitney peered over his shoulder. " 'Dr. Purvey's Celebrated Pills For Curing Rheumatism, Asthma, and Dyspepsia,' " she read. The boys roared with laughter.

"Oh, look at this china," Mrs. Whitney continued, burrowing into another trunk. "Most of it's broken, though. What a shame. And look! Candles! It's a miracle they didn't all melt away in that hot barn. They certainly are big, aren't they? Oh!" The candle fell from her hand and rolled into the dust. "Goodness, it's heavy."

Heavy! "Mom, let me see that candle," Pete said.

She handed it to him, watching curiously as he

91

lifted it in his hand, as if estimating its weight. "That's it!" he shouted. "Danny, let me use your knife."

Bewildered, Danny handed it over and Pete gouged the wax. Suddenly the knife made a scraping sound. Pete grinned and held up the candle.

Instead of a wick, the candle had a core of gold!

11

"**O**h, Pete!" Mrs. Whitney gasped.

Danny and Duffy each grabbed a candle and began to scrape at the old wax. In moments, each had revealed a center of gold.

"Why, there must be dozens of these candles!" Mrs. Whitney said, burrowing through the contents of the trunks.

"How did you know?" Danny said, staring at Pete in awe. "How did you guess?"

"Is this it?" Duffy demanded. "Those candles! Is that where he hid the treasure?"

Pete shook his head. "No, there has to be more. Don't forget, he collected jewels and paper money, too. You see, the captain never intended to take the treasure to the South. He had the whole thing planned in advance, right down to the day he'd leave town.

"He never thought he'd be caught by the people in Oak Bluff. He figured they'd be so busy with the celebration, they wouldn't know he was gone until late that night or maybe the next morning. By then, he'd have had a good head start. But he was going to be traveling the back roads for a while, and some of that country must have been pretty rough. What if he got stopped by bandits? He wanted it to look like he was a poor peddler, so no one would bother him. He had to hide the treasure where no one would think of looking."

Pete took a breath, then went on. "He melted down the gold jewelry after he'd taken the jewels out. He hid the paper money, too. We'll have to go through everything in these trunks and try to guess where he could have hidden the rest of the treasure. Remember, anything that seems heavy may have gold in it."

"I wonder," Mrs. Whitney murmured. She picked up the taffeta dress again and looked at it suspiciously. Then she began to run her hands over the seams. When she reached the hem, she yelped, "Eureka!"

"Let me see, Mom," Pete said. He reached for the dress.

"No, Pete, let me do it. You're too rough. This dress is a museum piece."

"But, Mom —"

"No! It's my turn." Carefully she cut the stitches with Danny's knife. Then she shook the fabric, and a small handful of jewels — garnets, pearls, even a small cameo — rolled into her hand. Duffy gave a low whistle.

Now that they knew what to look for, the trunks were searched. It was Duffy who found the stack of Bibles at the bottom of one trunk. The ones at the bottom appeared to have warped covers. Carefully Pete loosened a corner of the paper that covered the front cover. Beneath lay a thin stack of aging bills in various denominations.

"That's not all," Pete said. "Mom, remember that box of old irons you showed me?"

"The sadirons? What about them?"

"There was a kettle in that box, and it was so heavy Jessica could hardly lift it. I'll bet you anything it's got a lining of gold. And there may be more kettles like it!"

Mrs. Whitney sat down on one of the trunks very suddenly. "I feel weak," she said. "This has all happened so fast! Pete, I can't believe we found — *you* found — the missing treasure! But how did you figure it out?"

Pete grinned. "It's a long story," he said. Then he paused. How could he explain his experiences in Zeb's body? Zeb, after all, had given Pete the final clue.

"Well?" Duffy demanded. "So tell us!"

Pete took a deep breath. "Before I get into that, I want to check out that kettle we have in the house. And I'm thirsty, Mom. Can't we have a cold drink?"

"Good idea!" Mrs. Whitney led the way into the kitchen and began pouring lemonade while the boys examined the kettle. It certainly was heavy, as heavy as Pete remembered. Duffy peered into it. Then, with the tip of the knife, he scraped at the bottom. Sure enough, paint flaked away, revealing something shiny.

"Look at that!" Danny breathed. "He just put a layer of paint over it!"

"Sure," Pete said. "It was just to disguise it long enough for him to get away."

"Okay, Pete, now you have to tell us how you thought of all this," Duffy reminded him.

"Well, to begin with, like Mom said, I was determined to find that treasure. But I didn't believe it had been buried. That didn't make any sense. Why go to all the trouble of getting it and then burying it?"

"I told you, they thought he planned to come back for it," Danny argued. "Since the wagon had been searched, that was the only logical conclusion."

"It was logical," Pete admitted, "but if the captain had buried the treasure he would have had to return to dig it up. And that was taking too big a risk. Once people knew he'd stolen it, they'd be looking for him. He needed to get as far away as possible. Besides, if he had buried it, why did he bother to leave with his wagon?"

"I don't get it," Danny said. "What does that have to do with it? All his things were in that wagon. He was a peddler."

"A peddler who didn't have any luck selling his stuff because everything he carried in his wagon could be bought in stores. You told me that when he arrived in Oak Bluff, he was really down on his luck, and he had a beat-up old wagon and a lame horse."

"But I still — "

"This morning Packy Coates said the captain stole Mrs. Hatler's horse, remember?"

"Yeah, but — "

"Don't you see? If he'd buried the treasure, he could have ridden out of here on one horse. But he took his wagon and his horse *and* Mrs. Hatler's horse. Two horses would give him a lot of speed, but the townspeople caught up with him pretty quickly. That's because the wagon was so heavy. *And the only thing that could make it that heavy was gold!*"

"Wow!" Danny said. "But why didn't the townspeople see that?"

"Because they were angry," Pete said. "The captain made fools of them."

"But you still haven't explained how you figured out where to look," Mrs. Whitney said.

"To tell the truth," Pete grinned, "I wasn't really sure. The fact is, I had a bunch of clues, but it wasn't until today that I finally put them all together."

"Like what?" Duffy said.

"A few days ago when Dad and I were looking in one of the sheds, he pointed out some little clay pots that he called crucibles. He said they were for melting metal, but he didn't know what the Hatlers would have done with them. I didn't even realize it then, but that was the first clue.

"Another clue was that heavy kettle. The next clue was when Packy mentioned the two horses. Remember, Danny? He said that Zeb Tyler had gotten really sick after the Fourth, and while he was hallucinating, he talked about the Widow Hatler's stolen horse. Packy said Zeb probably didn't even see the treasure, but I bet he did. He didn't care about the horse; he was trying to tell people *why* the captain had stolen the horse."

A light dawned in Danny's eyes and he nodded. But Mrs. Whitney had a funny expression on her face, as if she thought Pete was leaving something out. To distract her, Pete hurried on.

"You gave me the final clue, Mom."

"Me? What did I do?"

"When I couldn't find my camera," Pete explained to the other boys, "Mom pointed out that it was right under my nose. I was looking for the camera, not the box it was in. Mom said that sometimes people do that. They look right at something and never see it because they are looking for it in a different form. That's when I knew!

"You see," Pete went on, "the people were so angry and upset, they weren't thinking. They were looking for the things they'd given him: the rings and watches and stuff like that. They didn't realize he'd changed it all by melting down the gold and hiding the jewels in a different place!"

"And once they started tearing Mrs. Hatler's place apart, I'm sure she was pretty upset, too," Mrs. Whitney added. "She probably never let anyone else look for the treasure after that."

"That's right!" Danny said. "That's exactly what happened."

"I'm surprised Mrs. Hatler didn't try to sell the things in the wagon," Mrs. Whitney said. "She would have been entitled to some compensation, I'm sure."

Pete grinned. "But Mom, remember that awful purple dress? You said yourself, who'd wear a thing like that?"

"But Mrs. Hatler must have gone through those trunks looking for things she could use. After all, we didn't find that kettle in the wagon, remember?"

"Yeah, but once she tried lifting it, she probably had second thoughts," Pete said. "But it would have been funny, wouldn't it, if she'd tried to use that kettle and didn't know it had gold in the bottom."

"Or what if she needed those candles?" Danny gasped. "She'd have found it right away."

"As for the Bibles," Mrs. Whitney said, "each family had its own, passed down from one generation to the next. They were often used to record births, deaths, and marriages. In fact, the Hatler family Bible is still in the house. I found it after we moved in. But I'm surprised she didn't throw the rest of the things away — or give them away."

"But the Hatlers never got rid of anything," Pete reminded her. "From the time we moved in, we said that over and over. And that was another clue. If the treasure wasn't buried, it had to be here because — "

" — the Hatlers never threw anything away!" Danny and Duffy roared in unison. They all laughed.

"Well," Mrs. Whitney said, "I'm going to call your dad, Pete. I can hardly wait to see his face when he sees what you found!"

"Jessica's not going to believe this, either," Pete said.

"What are you going to do with the treasure?" Danny asked.

"I don't know," Pete said. Not long ago he remembered thinking that if he found the treasure he would try to persuade his family to move back to the city. Now that didn't seem to be important.

"Boy, are you gonna be rich," Duffy said enviously.

"With the price of gold on today's market, I'd say that treasure is worth a fortune," Mrs. Whitney added. "Well, what *are* you going to do with it?"

Pete walked slowly to the kitchen door, staring out across the yard, deep in thought. The heat made everything shimmer. Suddenly Pete blinked and stared! For a moment, he thought he saw the ghostly silhouette of a boy wearing a battered felt hat, barefoot, with a scrap of bandage around one toe. He blinked again in disbelief and the vision disappeared.

Zeb Tyler? Saying good-bye? Or was he trying to give Pete a final message?

Then all at once, Pete knew! He knew why Zeb had pulled him back in time and what the message was. He turned to the others. "The treasure doesn't belong to me," he said. "It never did. It really belongs to Oak Bluff. Captain Scalawag stole it from the people. It wouldn't be right for me to keep it."

Mrs. Whitney smiled. "I agree. That treasure could go a long way toward building something wonderful for the whole town to use. Maybe hospital equipment or something for the schools or even a roller rink!" She laughed. Then she added wistfully, "I wish the captain's victims could know that the treasure will be put to good use after all."

Pete thought about Zeb, and he couldn't help grinning. "Who knows, Mom. Maybe they do!"

About the Author

JANET LORIMER has written several children's books, including *The Biggest Bubble in the World*. Her inspiration for *The Mystery of the Missing Treasure* was a Civil War legend she first heard when she was fifteen and living in California. A former elementary school teacher, she lives in Ewa Beach, Hawaii, with her husband, two daughters, and a cat named Puffy who is very much a part of the family.

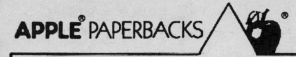

APPLE® PAPERBACKS

Pick an Apple and Polish Off Some Great Reading!

BEST-SELLING APPLE TITLES

☐ MT43944-8	**Afternoon of the Elves** Janet Taylor Lisle	**$2.75**
☐ MT43109-9	**Boys Are Yucko** Anna Grossnickle Hines	**$2.75**
☐ MT43473-X	**The Broccoli Tapes** Jan Slepian	**$2.95**
☐ MT42709-1	**Christina's Ghost** Betty Ren Wright	**$2.75**
☐ MT43461-6	**The Dollhouse Murders** Betty Ren Wright	**$2.75**
☐ MT43444-6	**Ghosts Beneath Our Feet** Betty Ren Wright	**$2.75**
☐ MT44351-8	**Help! I'm a Prisoner in the Library** Eth Clifford	**$2.75**
☐ MT44567-7	**Leah's Song** Eth Clifford	**$2.75**
☐ MT43618-X	**Me and Katie (The Pest)** Ann M. Martin	**$2.75**
☐ MT41529-8	**My Sister, The Creep** Candice F. Ransom	**$2.75**
☐ MT42883-7	**Sixth Grade Can Really Kill You** Barthe DeClements	**$2.75**
☐ MT40409-1	**Sixth Grade Secrets** Louis Sachar	**$2.75**
☐ MT42882-9	**Sixth Grade Sleepover** Eve Bunting	**$2.75**
☐ MT41732-0	**Too Many Murphys** Colleen O'Shaughnessy McKenna	**$2.75**